GameQuest

PLAYER VS. PLAYER

GAME

QUEST

PLAYER VS. PLAYER

ASH J. WU

Scholastic Inc.

If you purchased this book without a cover, you should be aware that this book is stolen property. It was reported as "unsold and destroyed" to the publisher, and neither the author nor the publisher has received any payment for this "stripped book."

Text and illustrations copyright © 2025 by Ash J. Wu

All rights reserved. Published by Scholastic Inc., *Publishers since 1920*. SCHOLASTIC and associated logos are trademarks and/or registered trademarks of Scholastic Inc.

The publisher does not have any control over and does not assume any responsibility for author or third-party websites or their content.

No part of this publication may be reproduced, stored in a retrieval system, or transmitted in any form or by any means, electronic, mechanical, photocopying, recording, or otherwise, or used to train any artificial intelligence technologies, without written permission of the publisher. For information regarding permission, write to Scholastic Inc., Attention: Permissions Department, 557 Broadway, New York, NY 10012.

This book is a work of fiction. Names, characters, places, and incidents are either the product of the author's imagination or are used fictitiously, and any resemblance to actual persons, living or dead, business establishments, events, or locales is entirely coincidental.

ISBN 978-1-5461-0107-9

10 9 8 7 6 5 4 3 2 1   25 26 27 28 29

Printed in the U.S.A.   40

First printing 2025

Book design by Maithili Joshi

CHAPTER 1

"The zombies are getting closer!" Tai shouted.

Kat, Alex, and Tai were in the woods, surrounded by a mob of hungry zombies. Just an average Friday morning.

Average, because the three friends were playing Otherworld, their favorite of the Game Quest video games.

"I've got this one!" Tai said, slashing a zombie with their sword. The zombie fell backward and faded away. But another zombie was approaching Tai from behind.

"Watch out, Tai!" Alex swooped down from the sky, on the back of an albatrossaur. The beast kicked its talons at the zombie, knocking it to the ground.

"AH! Get that thing away from me!" cried Tai.

"The zombie? I just did," said Alex.

"Not that; I mean that thing you're riding on! Keep it away from me. It's creepy!" said Tai as another zombie

approached them. They quickly defeated it with a diagonal slash.

"His name is Barry," said Alex, patting the

albatrossaur like a dog. "Don't listen to them, Barry."

"Hey, guys, check this out!" Kat called as the zombies wandered into her trap. When enough of them had gathered, Kat pulled the lever next to her. A giant spring hidden under the zombies catapulted them high into the air.

"Did you guys see that? I call it the KAT-apult! Get it?" Kat turned to her friends, but Alex and Tai were busy fighting off zombies of their own.

"You weren't watching?" Kat asked with a frown.

"Sorry! Busy kicking zombie butt over here!" said Tai, hacking them left and right. "Well, kicking butt with a sword. Slashing butt?" Tai climbed into a tree to get some height, then jumped down in an aerial sword attack. The move took out four zombies at once.

"Oh yeah! Now THIS is how you play!" Tai did a victory dance. "You guys should be watching *me*. You could learn a few things . . . like why using weapons is the way to win this game!"

Kat and Alex rolled their eyes.

"Me and Barry have been defeating loads of zombies without ANY weapons," said Alex.

Kat crossed her arms. "If you guys had bothered to watch, you would've seen my trap defeat more zombies than your sword attack OR Barry did," she said.

"No way! I just took out like ten zombies at once!" said Tai.

"It was four," Kat corrected them. Alex laughed at Tai's overconfidence.

"Four . . . ten . . . What does it matter? I'm unstoppable!" said Tai.

"And bad at counting," whispered Alex to Barry.

Tai smirked and crouched with their sword. "Here, watch this! I'll take out twenty with this move!"

Tai whirled their sword around like a tornado.

"Spinning attack!" shouted Tai, taking out one-two-three-four-five zombies. But then . . .

CLANG!

Tai's sword shattered into pieces... and disappeared.

"NO!" Tai yelled. "I've had this sword for ages, what gives?!"

"Did you forget about durability again?" Alex asked as Barry pecked at zombies. "All weapons break eventually... unless they're made of starstone."

Tai gulped. "Oh yeah. I sure could use some starstone right now..." The zombies surrounded Tai.

"Hold on!" called Alex, flying through the air toward Tai. "Barry, use your wings!"

Barry stretched out and began to flap with all his might. A huge gust of air pushed the zombie mob back. But soon Barry began to slow down. Moments later, the albatrossaur landed on the ground, panting.

"Barry, what's wrong?!" asked Alex, checking over the creature. "Oh no, his stamina ran out!"

Just as the zombies were closing in...

Meanwhile, Kat was busy setting her next zombie trap in a nearby stone tower she had built earlier in the day. "Hey, guys, you've got to see this!" she called from inside the tower. When there was no reply, she headed outside to look for her friends, but they had disappeared. All that was left were blocks of materials from their inventory. GAME OVER.

Kat gasped. The mob of zombies was now staggering toward her. She knew she had to act quickly, or she would meet the same fate as Alex and Tai.

Kat ran back through the tower's entrance and pulled the wooden lever at the bottom of the stairs.

A large stone door slammed down, squashing a zombie underneath it. Then she ran up the spiral staircase as the zombies pounded at the door.

When she reached the top of the tower, Kat waited by the second lever with a smirk. The brainless bunch of zombies was walking right into her trap.

They kept pounding until the stone door fell with a bang, then piled inside the tower.

Kat's fingers hovered over the handle of the lever. "Come on, just a little farther . . ." she said, waiting for all the zombies to gather on the staircase.

But for a long moment, they stood deadly still.

Kat raised an eyebrow and waved down at the zombies. "Uh, hello? Don't you guys want to eat me?"

The zombies slowly raised their heads and looked at Kat with glowing orange eyes. Suddenly, their whole bodies burst into flames.

Kat gasped. "Emberdead?!"

The zombies had evolved into emberdead—flaming creatures who were much faster than ordinary zombies. So fast that they were already halfway up the tower before Kat remembered her trap.

"Oh no you don't!" Kat quickly pulled on the wooden lever. A door within the tower opened, releasing a giant steel boulder that rolled down the stairs.

Kat watched with anticipation as the boulder went down the spiral staircase, rolling faster and faster. It reached the zombies, knocking down the first few like a giant bowling ball.

"Take that!" Kat cheered. But then her smile dropped.

The fire of the zombies rapidly began to melt the steel boulder, shrinking it down until it disappeared completely.

Kat was all out of traps. She looked over the edge of the tower. It was far too high to jump down. Desperately, she pulled at some loose stone blocks to throw at the emberdead.

It was no use. Though she knocked a few over, there were too many of them, and she quickly ran out of blocks. There was nowhere to escape to.

One final, desperate idea crossed Kat's mind . . . but could she pull it off?

CHAPTER 2

In Ada Lovelace Elementary's computer lab, Alex and Tai watched as the emberdead surrounded Kat on-screen.

"Bad luck," said Tai.

BAD LUCK...

Alex nodded. "Yeah, I heard the chances of zombies evolving into emberdead are rare."

Kat watched them attack and drain the hit points of her avatar. If she didn't do something quick, the tower she'd spent so much time on was toast. She just needed to wait for the right moment . . .

Tai spun on their swivel chair. "Well, at least we're all in the same boat. I lost my awesome sword and Alex's big goofy bird is gone—"

"His name was Barry," Alex sighed, hanging his head. "It took me so long to tame him."

Kat's hit points continued to drain. Her eyes darted between the screen and her friends.

"Big bird, Barry, same thing. Hey, at least it'll respawn somewhere. Why did you name it anyway?" asked Tai.

Alex frowned. "What's wrong with that? You name your silly attacks."

Tai crossed their arms. "Hey, my attacks are cool! Way cooler than any bird!"

"They are not!" said Alex.

Kat glanced at Alex and Tai. They weren't watching her. This was her chance.

Just before her health bar reached zero, Kat quickly pressed the computer's power button.

"Oh no!" Kat cried, jumping up from her chair. "What just happened? My screen went blank!"

"HUH?" Alex and Tai hurried over to Kat and stood around her computer.

Kat put her hands on her hips. "It must've been some kind of... power cut! I think there's a storm outside. Maybe that caused it?"

"Oh yeah. Maybe," said Tai, raising their eyebrows. "But if your game turned off, does that mean you got to keep all your stuff?"

Kat gathered up her notebook and pencils and

shoved them into her bag. "I'm not sure! I guess so! Hey, we'd better head to class. Don't want to miss our weekly performance!" Kat said, nudging Alex and Tai with her elbow.

"Oh no," Alex groaned. "I almost forgot."

"Same rules as last week?" said Tai with a grin. "Whoever laughs loses?"

The school bell rang. The three friends headed out of the computer lab and down the corridor. Alex paused to look out the window. Gray skies loomed over the ball field, but it wasn't raining. *No storm yet*, he thought to himself, then hurried after his friends.

In class, they stowed their backpacks and got ready to rock as Mr. Garcia waved them to the front of the room. Each of them held a different instrument: a drum, a recorder, and an accordion. Their band began to play, and all the other kids winced and covered their ears.

They sounded awful.

Why in the world Mr. Garcia let them perform every Friday morning was hard to understand, but Kat guessed it had to do with how passionately they played. That or Mr. Garcia just had terrible taste in music.

Kat wanted to cover her mouth to contain her giggles. She looked across at Alex and Tai. Tai's face was red from holding back laughter. Alex's mouth was a straight line. But it kept twitching—he was struggling not to grin.

Once the song was over, the trio high-fived one another and sat down.

"Thank you for that beautiful performance," said Mr. Garcia. "And now for a special announcement: Ada Lovelace Elementary will be hosting a charity fundraiser this year. It's going to be...." Mr. Garcia lowered his glasses and squinted at the piece of paper. "A Game Quest tournament."

The whole class erupted into enthusiastic chatter.

"Settle down, class." Mr. Garcia walked around the room, handing out the tournament rules and sign-up sheets. "The game we'll use is Otherworld. You can register as a single player or as a team. And you'll be allowed to use the computer labs to practice during breaks." He glanced at Tai sternly. "So long as you sit in your seats properly and keep the noise down."

Kat looked over the tournament rules.

She couldn't wait to get started! Kat glanced at Tai, whose grin stretched from ear to ear. They gave her a thumbs-up. But Alex wouldn't look at her.

Lucy, who sat next to Kat, leaned over to ask, "Are you going to team up with Tai and Alex?"

Kat smiled. "Of course!"

Only she couldn't help thinking something was off with Alex. He was staring out the window at the rain that had just started to come down.

GAME QUEST TOURNAMENT

Whoever collects the most points wins!
Entry fee $$$ Charity Donation!

RULES:
NO CHEAT CODES.
NO STEALING FROM OTHER PLAYERS.
CHARITY SERVER ONLY (CODE #H1R3AD3R)

Points:

Defeating an Enemy 100
Defeating a World Boss 10,000

Crafting:

Small Item 25
Medium Item 100
Large Item 500

Befriending a Creature 200
Evolving a Creature 3,000

Inventory:

Starstone 10,000
Starstone Piece 5,000

But the rest of the school day was so busy, she didn't have a chance to ask him what was wrong. When the last bell rang, Kat, Alex, and Tai all returned to the computer lab. They loaded up Otherworld and joined the special competition server. This meant none of them had anything in their inventory.

Kat showed them her sign-up sheet. "I put us down as a team, so you don't need to bother filling in the form."

Tai grinned. "Oh, neat, thanks!"

"We could even think of a cool team name for ourselves!" Kat joked.

Alex stayed silent for a few moments, eyebrows furrowed. Then he asked quietly, "Kat, why did you lie earlier?"

"Wh-what?" stammered Kat.

"You said the storm turned your game off, but it only just started to rain a little while ago," said Alex, pointing at the skylights. The clouds were dark, and the heavy rainfall was loud on the glass.

Tai gasped. "HEY... Alex is right! That's not fair!"

Kat's face heated with embarrassment. "It... it happened on its own! And even if I was lying, you said it yourself: It was bad luck the emberdead showed up. I wanted to save everything I worked hard to make..."

"But Alex and I lost stuff and *we* didn't reset the game!" said Tai.

A flash of lightning lit up the computer lab.

Kat avoided eye contact.

"Just admit you made a mistake, Kat," said Alex.

"*I* made a mistake? You guys are the ones who forgot about durability and stamina!" Kat argued. "Besides, it's not my fault that my way of playing is the best," she blurted out, then cringed. "I mean..."

"WHAT?!" cried Alex and Tai.

"If my sword hadn't broken, I could've saved you both!" Tai said.

Alex groaned. "You guys only care about yourselves. I don't want to enter the competition with *either* of you!"

Lightning flashed outside, followed by another rumble of thunder.

Tai and Kat stared at Alex in shock.

"W-well, I don't want to enter with you guys

either!" Tai declared. Another rumble of thunder shook the room.

Teary-eyed, Kat grabbed the sign-up sheet.

"FINE, that settles it, then! I'm winning that tournament *alone*!" she said, then tore the sign-up sheet into pieces.

The moment that the paper split, a massive bolt of lightning struck the ground outside, accompanied by a deafening boom of thunder.

Everything went dark . . .

Kat felt herself falling. When she opened her eyes, she saw a bright blue sky filled with pixelated clouds.

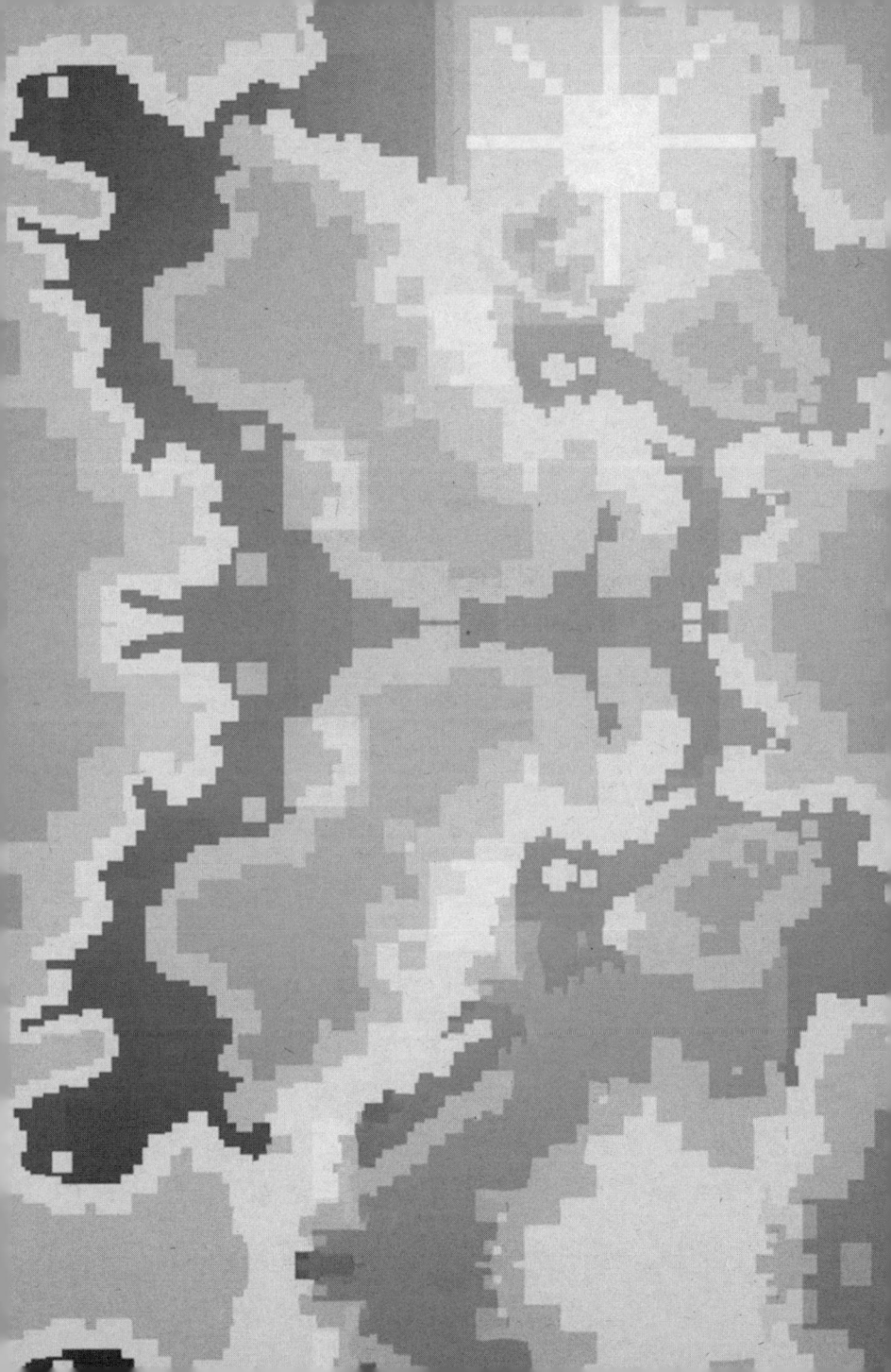

Pixelated clouds . . . like in . . . Otherworld?
Then suddenly . . . **SPLASH!**
Everything fell dark once again.

CHAPTER 3

Kat woke up on a golden beach. She coughed, then looked down at her hands.

"No way..." she gasped. They looked just like her Otherworld character's did!

She stood up and looked around. Farther along the beach, she spotted two blocky figures getting up from the ground. Kat recognized the avatars immediately.

"Tai! Alex!" Kat ran over to them.

"Kat!" said Tai and Alex.

For a few moments, they just stared at one another with shocked pixelated faces.

Then they burst into laughter.

"Your faces are too funny!" Tai laughed.

"So is yours, Tai!" said Kat.

"I can't believe this. We're in Otherworld . . ." said Alex breathlessly.

"But how did we get here?" Kat asked. "And how do we get out?"

She turned around and spotted a mountain range in the distance. A castle sat on the tallest peak, with dark clouds swirling around it. And high above that castle was a giant, glowing portal.

"That's gotta be where we came from."

"So, if this is anything like the game, I guess we just need to go on a quest and get through that portal?" said Tai. "As much as I love Otherworld, I already miss having fingers." Tai held out their block hands.

"It's pretty far away..." said Alex quietly.

"I'm sure we can get there if we all work together!" said Kat. Then she paused and added, "We should work together, right?"

A silence fell as they all remembered their argument.

"Yeah," Alex mumbled.

Tai folded their arms. "Sure."

Kat nodded awkwardly. "Cool, cool, cool. So we should probably—"

A loud squawk interrupted Kat. Alex's head spun around at the familiar sound.

"Barry?!" cried Alex. Farther up the beach, a giant albatrossaur perched on a log. But unlike Barry, whose feathers were all white, this bird had wings with gray tips.

Alex ran toward it.

"Wait!" cried Kat, hurrying after him.

"That big bird looks even *bigger* than the original big bird," said Tai as they reluctantly followed.

The albatrossaur was at least one and a half times the size of Barry. She stared down at Alex with piercing yellow eyes. Alex reached out to pet her, but the bird snapped her beak at him.

"I knew that was a bad idea," said Tai.

"It's not a problem. We just need to find some food to tame her with," said Alex.

Kat stared at the albatrossaur. While Barry had friendly eyes, this one glared constantly.

"I don't know, Alex. It looks like it might take *a lot* of food to tame this one," said Kat. She squinted at the faraway portal. "We should focus on making something to launch us up there." Kat picked up a stick and began to draw in the sand. "I'll design something. You guys should look for materials to craft with."

Tai nodded and headed down the beach. But after finding a single stick, they got distracted thinking of all the monsters they might come across.

With another squawk, the albatrossaur flew off into the distance. Alex stared after her with a frown. Then he headed for some nearby trees. Maybe they'd have some fruit he could use to get her back.

A few minutes later, Kat finished her catapult design. "Hey, guys! Feel free to bring over whatever you've found!" She glanced over her shoulder. Alex was currently halfway up a mango tree and Tai was swinging their stick around like a sword.

Kat groaned and slapped her forehead. "Guess I'm the only one doing something useful around here."

She stood up and went to search the beach for materials herself. Moments later, she came across a flint block, four wooden blocks, two iron blocks, and three stone blocks, all hidden under the shadow of a palm tree. Kat gathered all the pieces. Though it wouldn't be enough to craft her catapult, it was a good start.

But then a sparkle under the sand caught Kat's eye. She began to dig. Her eyebrows shot up when she realized what she'd found: a *starstone*.

"Wow... I could make anything with this!" Kat

whispered to herself. "Hey, guys—" She started to call over the others, but stopped herself. The glittering starstone in her hands was worth ten thousand points in the competition. If she kept it, she would definitely win.

Her friends hadn't listened to her at all. Alex was picking mangoes from the trees. And Tai was lying on the beach, taking a break from fighting imaginary zombies. Neither of them were gathering crafting materials.

Kat narrowed her eyes and made her decision, pocketing the starstone.

By the time Alex had gathered a bunch of fruit, the albatrossaur had flown over the horizon and out of sight. He sighed and kicked a stone. It bounced in between two curved palm trees. When Alex looked closer, he saw that hidden behind those trees was the entrance to a cave.

"Hey, guys! Over here!" Alex called to Kat and Tai.

"Ooh, I bet there's a ton of stuff we can use in there!" said Kat.

"Or maybe even some monsters to fight!" Tai rushed inside, ahead of the others.

"Wait up!" cried Alex. He and Kat hurried into the cave after Tai.

Inside, the tunnel was dark, damp, and smelled of seawater. Kat, Alex, and Tai went in different directions and searched for anything interesting.

"Did anyone find any useful materials?" Tai called out.

"I found some flint, wood, iron, and stone," said Kat.

Tai spun around to face her. "Wow, that's great! I should make a weapon in case we come across an enemy. I'll take the wood, iron, and stone!" Tai held out a hand expectantly.

"Hold on! I need those to craft my catapult. You can have a couple blocks of wood, but that's it," said Kat. She handed over two of the blocks to Tai.

Tai took them and crafted the only weapon they could make—a flimsy wooden sword. "No fair," they said, pouting. "You're hogging everything."

"Hey, I found all this stuff myself!" replied Kat, combining another wood block and flint to make a torch. "You both should have been collecting materials

when I asked you to."

"I couldn't find anything," said Tai.

Kat's mouth hung open. "You didn't even look! You were playing around with a stick!"

"I was practicing in case of an ambush!!"

"Guys, be quiet!" Alex hushed them. His eyes were wide as he pointed ahead. "What is that?"

A large shadow was coming around the corner . . .

CHAPTER 4

"An ambush! Get behind me!" shouted Tai.

The shadow grew closer and closer, until the creature leaped around the corner in front of them...

"An ornabun!" Alex gasped in excitement. "She's so cute!"

Tai lowered their sword. "Nice! We should take the rubies from its antlers. You can craft fireproof stuff with them!"

"Oh yeah, those could come in handy," said Kat. "Especially if we run into emberdead again."

She shivered at the thought.

"Wait!" Alex stood in front of the ornabun protectively. "If you take her rubies, she won't be able to evolve."

Tai shrugged. "So?"

"Ornabun evolve into ornadeer. You can ride them, and they have unlimited stamina," explained Alex.

"That also sounds good," Kat said. "How long does evolving them take?"

"It depends on their bond with the player." Alex took a mango from his inventory and held it toward the ornabun. Her nose twitched, then she hopped over and took the fruit.

"See, we're already bonding!" said Alex.

"Hmm, all right, I guess," said Kat, watching the creature eat. "We'll keep her for now."

Alex frowned. "'For now'?"

Tai tapped the blade of their sword on the ground. "There's no point in keeping her if she isn't useful."

Alex put his hands on his hips. "I just told you she could become an ornadeer! Weren't you listening?" he asked.

Tai shrugged. "I've never heard of an ornadeer. Did you just make that up because you want to keep her?"

"Ornadeer are real!" Alex shouted, spooking the little furball. She struggled out of Alex's arms and scampered farther into the cave.

"Amby! Come back!" cried Alex.

"You already named it?!" asked Tai.

"Uh . . . guys?" Kat pointed at the ceiling, a look of alarm on her face. "There's something up there!"

It was a giant venomous snafox. And it was slithering toward them.

Tai held their sword out. "I'll handle this. You guys keep moving ahead!"

Alex ran in the direction that Amby had gone. When he caught up to the creature, she was shivering in the corner of the cave.

"I'm sorry I shouted," said Alex, holding out another mango. "Tai can be so annoying . . ."

Amby stared at Alex for a moment before coming closer to eat the fruit.

Alex very gently patted her on the head. "I'm going to protect you," he whispered. Amby squeaked happily.

Meanwhile, Tai slashed at the snafox. It hissed and lunged at them, but they dodged out of the way. When Tai spun and struck again, the creature flinched, then whacked Tai with its tail, knocking them back.

"Oof!" exclaimed Tai, clutching their stomach. "This stupid sword isn't strong enough..."

Kat watched the fight from a distance. Alex reappeared and headed over to her, now with Amby in his arms.

"Tai needs help," said Kat. She checked her inventory, then crafted a basic slingshot. "There we go!" she said proudly. But then she paused. "I don't have any ammo..."

Alex looked around, using the glow of Amby's horns to light the way. He spotted a pile of stones. "Here!" said Alex, handing them to Kat. "You can use these."

"Thanks!" said Kat. She loaded the slingshot and fired one stone after another at the snafox. This time, instead of flinching, the beast pulled back, the combination of Tai's attacks and the stones doing extra damage.

Tai glared at Kat. "I can handle this by myself!"

"But we can defeat it together!" said Kat. She kept shooting at the snafox until she ran out of ammunition. "Alex, more stones, please!"

With the help of Amby's glowing horns, Alex gathered all the ones he could see and gave them to Kat.

"I can defeat this snafox on my own!" protested Tai, using a spin attack to slow the creature. But during Tai's last hit, their sword shattered on impact.

"Snap!" cursed Tai, now defenseless.

Kat quickly loaded the slingshot and fired until it shattered, too. Luckily, her strikes drained the last of the snafox's energy. It slammed onto its scaly side and disappeared.

"We defeated it!" cheered Alex.

"Thanks to my quick thinking." Kat smirked, folding her arms.

Tai frowned. "If you'd given me the materials you'd used for that slingshot, I could've made a better sword. I wouldn't have needed your help!"

"Well, it all worked out fine, so it doesn't matter, right?" asked Kat.

Tai muttered grumpily and stomped ahead.

Kat and Alex exchanged a look.

They followed Tai through the cave until they found an exit. Outside, a steep hill stretched down into a forest.

"Where to next?" asked Kat.

Tai scowled and looked around. Then their eyebrows shot up. "Look! Windmills!"

Sure enough, several small green windmills were hidden among the trees, along with a cluster of houses with thatched roofs.

"A village!" said Alex. He looked down at Amby. "Have you ever been to one before?"

"WOOHOO!" cheered Tai. "A village has got to have a craft shop—which means I can make better weapons than that terrible wooden sword!!"

Tai sprinted toward the village. They tripped midway down the hill, did a roll, got back up, and kept running. "I'm okay!" they shouted over their shoulder.

Relieved Tai was back to normal, Kat and Alex laughed and hurried after them.

But though the questers didn't know it, they were being followed . . .

CHAPTER 5

As Kat, Alex, and Tai wandered closer to the village, they spotted something they definitely did NOT want to see.

"What a weird sign," said Kat.

"What?!" Tai hung their head. "This village doesn't have any villagers? Or supplies? Then why should we go there?"

Alex raised an eyebrow. "I don't think that sign is right. I can literally see people from here."

He was right. When they reached the village, it was bustling with people.

Amby's eyes went wide. She wriggled in Alex's arms.

"I don't think Amby likes it here," said Alex. "Can we leave?"

"Look, a craft stall!" said Tai, ignoring Alex and running ahead.

Kat hurried after them. Alex sighed, then followed.

The craft stall sold only basic materials, but they were all incredibly useful.

"I could make so many weapons with this stuff!" said Tai, jumping up and down.

But Kat was confused. "Why did the sign outside your village say that no one lives here and that you don't have materials?" she asked the shopkeeper.

"You don't know about the Craft King?" The shopkeeper looked around to make sure no one was listening. "He's been raiding all of the villages in

Otherworld and stealing their craft materials."

"Hey, remember the score sheet?" Tai whispered to Kat. "This Craft King sounds like a boss—we'll get ten thousand points if we defeat him."

Kat smiled. That many points would go a long way toward winning the competition.

The shopkeeper stared into the distance with a wide-eyed look. "If the Craft King found us, it would be game over for our village. We wouldn't be able to build schools or mix medicinal potions or—"

"Yeah, cool. Anyway..." interrupted Tai. "We'd like to buy all your materials!" Tai turned to Kat. "You've got coins, right? Or anything we can sell? More wood blocks, maybe?"

Kat knew the starstone in her pocket would probably sell for thousands of coins. But it was worth way more than that—ten thousand points in the competition!

"No." Kat looked away from Tai. "I've got nothing to sell."

"All right, so we can't buy anything," Alex said as Amby wriggled in his arms. "We should go, right?"

Tai glanced at Amby. "How many coins would you give us for our ornabun?" Tai asked the shopkeeper excitedly.

"That's a rare find. I'll buy it for five hundred coins," replied the shopkeeper.

Alex's jaw dropped. "She's NOT for sale!" He glared at Tai.

"Fine . . . That leaves me one last option," Tai said

with a smirk. "What about a DUEL TRADE? If I beat you in a fight, I can have all the materials for free!"

"I forgot you could do that," said Kat. "Great idea, Tai! But what will you fight with?"

"My fists," Tai said, kissing each knuckle. "So, what do you say?"

The shopkeeper stared at Tai, then pulled out a giant claymore sword from behind the counter. "Do you really think you can beat me?"

Tai's jaw dropped. Then they pointed at Amby. "Are you sure we can't sell that thing?" Tai asked.

"OF COURSE I'm sure!" snapped Alex.

Tai threw their hands up in the air. "Fine, no materials for us!" they mumbled, and stormed off.

Kat put a hand on Alex's shoulder. "I'm sure Tai will calm down in a minute. Let's go check out the rest of the village."

While their friends wandered through the market, Tai walked alone down the cobblestone street, their hands in their pockets. Alex and Kat never cared what Tai thought about anything, and this time was no different.

As they passed an alleyway, a voice called out.

"Pssst... Hey, kid. Over here."

A cat in a pointed hat beckoned to Tai. "I saw what happened to you at that stall. I've been there," said the cat. "No money, no power . . . bad luck."

Tai sighed and walked over. "Yeah. If I was able to sell that orna-whatever, I could've crafted a great weapon for me and my friends!"

The cat nodded as she tapped her wand against the cobblestones. "I get it. You want to protect them, but they won't support you. Well, today you're in luck. Your friend Witchat here supports you, and I'd like to offer you a gift."

Tai pulled a face. "It's not a hair ball or dead mouse or something, is it?"

"No," said Witchat. "It's something way more useful and far less gross . . ."

Witchat waved her wand, and an incredible sword appeared in Tai's hands.

"WHOA!" Tai gasped. "This sword's stats are AMAZING! You're just GIVING this to me?"

"That's right," said Witchat. "There is no enemy this sword cannot beat. It's the most powerful sword in Otherworld. And there is absolutely NO catch..." Witchat's voice dropped to a whisper. "Except for draining your stamina with every use."

"What was that?" asked Tai. "I missed that last part."

"Don't worry about it," said Witchat, ushering Tai out of the alley. "Go challenge that shopkeeper and get all the materials you need!"

"Thanks so much!" said Tai. They paused. "Wait, you're not a witch, are you?"

"Oh, no way." Witchat shook her head, her pointy hat swiveling.

Tai squinted at her. "I mean, the wand, the broom, the pointy hat . . ." they said, scratching their head.

"Absolutely not." Witchat waved her hands dismissively. "This is a fairy wand. I carry the broom because I just LOVE sweeping. And the pointy hat hides an embarrassing growth on my head."

Tai stared at Witchat for a moment longer, then smiled. "Okay, cool! Thanks again!" Tai waved, then ran back toward the craft shop.

Kat and Alex were at a food stall when Tai zoomed past.

"Tai?!" called Kat.

She and Alex hurried after Tai, who was already deep in conversation with the shopkeeper.

"So if I win, I get all the materials you have in stock," said Tai. "And if you win . . ."

"I get every item your party has on hand—including the ornabun," confirmed the shopkeeper.

"DEAL!" said Tai, shaking the shopkeeper's hand.

"Tai!! What are you doing?!" cried Alex.

Kat's eyes were wide. Every item? If Tai lost, she'd lose the starstone!

"Don't do this, Tai!" Kat pleaded.

Tai grinned, revealing their new sword. "Don't worry, guys, everything is going to be okay. Look at this beauty!"

Amby recoiled at the sight of the sword.

The shopkeeper, wielding his giant claymore, walked around to the front of the market stall. "All right, kid, you asked for it!"

A giant countdown clock appeared in the sky.

3...

2...

1...

FIGHT!

CHAPTER 6

Tai locked blades with the shopkeeper, sending sparks flying.

Kat and Alex watched, fists clenched and eyes wide.

"Where did they get that sword from?!" asked Kat.

"No idea, but they'd better win," replied Alex through gritted teeth, hugging Amby tightly.

"You've got no chance, shopkeeper!" declared Tai loudly.

The shopkeeper drew back and swiftly slashed his sword down. Tai dodged just in time.

Kat covered her eyes and peeked out between

her fingers. "That sword could cut Tai in two if they're not careful!!" she squeaked.

But Tai's attacks and speed slowed the shopkeeper down. Finally, Tai managed to knock the shopkeeper's sword to the ground.

Kat cheered and Alex sighed in relief.

"That's some sword you got there," grumbled the shopkeeper.

"Well? What about all those materials?" Tai panted. "A deal's a deal."

"Fine," said the shopkeeper. "At least this will save me a visit from the Craft King . . ." He led Tai back to his stall and gave them all the craft materials he had. "You'll want to travel carefully," the shopkeeper warned. "The Craft King has eyes everywhere."

"Got it." Tai was still breathless. "We'll look around for any eyes."

"I don't think he meant that literally," said Kat with a smirk.

As the kids left the village and continued in the direction of the portal, Tai counted up all the craft materials they'd gained from their win.

"That's five steel blocks, ten iron blocks, and twenty wood blocks. Not bad for just one fight!" said Tai.

"That's great!" said Kat. "But next time, don't bet all our stuff without asking us first!"

Tai shrugged. "I knew I was going to win. And obviously"—Tai yawned—"things worked out for the best, so there's no reason to complain."

Kat rolled her eyes. Tai was repeating what she had said back at the cave.

Alex glared but said nothing. Amby looked up at him with worried eyes as the gang walked through the woods. Soon they reached a clearing with a wide swampy river.

Alex and Kat stopped before they reached the river's edge. But Tai, eyes half lidded, walked straight into the river.

"Watch out!" cried Kat.

Tai tried to step back out, but one of their feet were stuck. Kat and Alex sighed and began to pull on Tai's arms, their feet covered in thick swamp mud.

"Ew! This stuff is sticky!!" said Tai, grimacing.

"Well, at least we know we can't just walk across," said Alex.

Kat looked across the river. "We'll need a boat . . . but not just any boat. It needs to be designed just right . . ." Kat began to brainstorm.

After coming up with a plan, she turned to Tai.

"Can I please use some of the materials you won? I'll forgive you for taking that risk if you say yes!" Kat pleaded.

"Yeah, sure." Tai yawned and handed over the materials. "I've got the best sword ever, so use what you want." Then Tai walked off to sit under a nearby tree.

"Hey, can I help with the boat?" asked Alex.

Kat paused. "Um, sure!" she said. "I'm going to start over here . . ." Kat began crafting a wooden raft.

"How about a steel steering wheel?" suggested Alex.

Kat paused what she was doing and shook her head. "We should save the steel for the propeller. Wood is better," she replied.

"Oh, okay . . ." Alex frowned, then asked, "Can we give it a mast?"

"I don't think it'll need one if it has a propeller," Kat pointed out.

Alex looked down at the craft materials and perked up. "Can I build a little bed for Amby?"

Kat shrugged. "Um, can Amby just sleep on the floor? I need the materials for crafting this boat."

Alex sighed. "Okay, fine, I give up . . ." he said quietly.

Kat gave Alex a weak smile. "How about you just leave this to me? You and Amby can patrol the area for danger," she suggested.

Alex gave a mock salute. Amby copied him.

"Aye, aye, captain . . ." Alex said, then spun on his heel and started walking alongside the river.

After a few minutes, he came across a partially sunken boat with marks on its side.

"That's kind of weird, isn't it, Amby?" said Alex.

But before the ornabun could respond, Alex's thoughts were interrupted by a loud snore coming from Tai's direction.

Alex narrowed his eyes, remembering Tai's bet. He walked over to Tai and nudged them with his foot. "Wake up," he said.

Tai startled awake. "Hey, yeah, what?" Tai's voice was groggy.

"Why aren't you helping?" asked Alex.

"I already helped. I got all those craft materials, remember?" Tai crossed their arms.

Alex glared down at the ground.

"Kat may have forgiven you for what you did, but I haven't," said Alex quietly. "If you'd lost, I would've had to give Amby away! Don't you even care about her?"

Alex glanced up at Tai, who had fallen asleep mid-conversation.

"UGH! You are so annoying!" shouted Alex.

Tai bolted upright. "What did I do now?!"

"Guys! My masterpiece is COMPLETE!" called Kat. She proudly displayed her creation. "What do you think?"

Alex stormed onto the boat without a word. Tai sleepily shuffled after him.

"Geez... you're welcome." Kat pouted before following them on board.

They traveled along the river under a sky streaked

with the sunset's orange and pink glow. Kat looked up at the colors in admiration. "Look how far we've come! We're closer than ever to the portal home," she said. "And we couldn't have gotten here without working together!"

Alex shrugged and didn't make eye contact. Tai gave a tired grunt in response.

Kat frowned. She checked her inventory and saw that she still had some of the materials left. "I know what'll cheer you up . . ." said Kat with a big grin. She crafted an instrument no one had ever seen before. It had a horn like a tuba that was connected to a bagpipe sack. "I call it . . . THE MONSTROSITY!" she declared.

Alex and Tai stared at Kat as she began to play . . .

It sounded . . . awful.

Alex and Tai couldn't help but laugh.

"So? Do you guys think I should ask Mr. Garcia if I can perform at school?" Kat asked between giggles.

Alex shook his head. "It's not bad enough yet!" he

said. Then he crafted some steel cymbals onto the Monstrosity.

Even Tai stood up and began adding their own ideas: bells and whistles.

Soon they had created a mixed-up instrument that three people could play.

"It's MONSTROSITY version 2.0! Ready?" Kat asked.

They all began to play the horrible instrument at once.

Now it sounded BEYOND awful. It wasn't long before they collapsed into giggles.

"Oh, Mr. Garcia is going to LOVE this!" cackled Tai.

But then Amby let out a loud squeak and pointed into the distance. A giant ghostly boat full of zombies floated around the river bend . . .

And it was headed straight for them!

CHAPTER 7

Kat hurried to the helm and desperately turned the wheel to avoid the zombies' ship, but it was too late. The zombies leaped onto Kat's boat. Their leader drew a sword, and the two others loaded their bows with arrows.

"Oh no . . . these guys must've sunk that boat I saw earlier," said Alex, holding Amby close.

Kat's jaw dropped. "You saw a sunken boat earlier?! Why didn't you say anything?!"

"W-well, I—" stuttered Alex, but Tai cut him off.

"I've got this!" said Tai, staggering to their feet and unsheathing their sword.

Amby recoiled at the sight. Alex looked down at her in concern.

Tai clashed swords with the lead zombie, sidestepping to avoid the arrows of his henchmen.

"I think you need to be careful with that sword!" Alex called out.

Tai looked over their shoulder at Alex and narrowly avoided being struck by an arrow. "Don't distract me right now. I'm busy protecting you guys!" snapped Tai, turning back to fight the zombies. But with every swing of their sword, Tai became slower and slower, their body swaying and rocking until . . .

WHOOMPH!

Tai collapsed on the ground.

"Tai!" shouted Kat.

"We need to do something!" Alex called. "Do you have any materials left?"

Kat shook her head. "No, I used everything for the boat!"

"EVERYTHING?" Alex slapped his forehead. "Then . . . we'll just have to use the boat!"

Kat's and Alex's eyes locked—they had the same idea. Together, they desperately began to pull off parts of the boat to attack the zombies with, throwing wooden blocks and iron blocks their way. Kat even threw the wheel of the boat at them like a Frisbee, striking the lead zombie in the head.

Although the leader staggered, it wasn't enough to defeat him. Slowly, the zombies backed the kids into a corner.

"Guys . . . I can't . . . move . . ." said Tai between heavy breaths.

"This is bad . . ." whimpered Alex, shielding Amby with his arms. Amby's eyes darted between Alex and the zombies.

Suddenly, the ornabun leaped out of Alex's arms and onto the ground.

"Amby?!" said Alex.

The zombies loomed over Amby, readying their weapons. But then they recoiled as a cocoon of sparkling light swirled around the ornabun.

When the light faded, Amby had transformed into an ornadeer!

"Whoa!!" said Alex in shock. "You evolved!"

"She looks totally different!" said Kat.

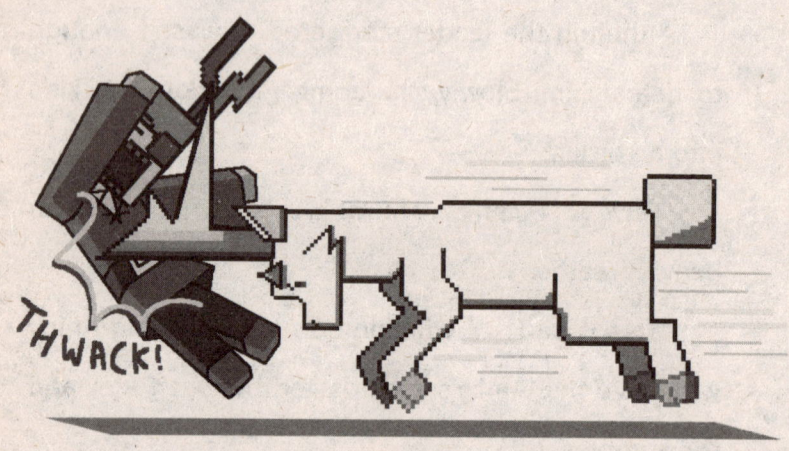

Amby charged at the zombies and attacked with her horns. She backed *them* into a corner, on the other side of the boat.

"Go, Amby!" cheered Kat and Alex.

One of the zombies fired an arrow that chipped a shard off Amby's horn.

"Oh no!" cried Alex. He ran and grabbed the shard off the ground.

With a final swing of her antlers, Amby knocked the zombies back into the swamp.

Kat picked up and reattached the ship's wheel, cranked the lever, and quickly steered the boat away.

Tai still lay flat on the ground, sword in hand.

"Amby, do you think we should get rid of that thing?" Alex whispered.

Amby huffed and trotted over to Tai's sword, raising a hoof above it to stamp on it . . .

"NO!" Tai cried, pointing the sword at Amby. "Don't you dare break it!"

"Don't YOU point that sword at her. She just saved us!" Alex said. "And she can sense something is wrong with that sword. Where did you even get it?!"

"A kind stranger with a pointy hat gave it to me!" Tai snapped, getting up to their feet. "And Amby only defeated those zombies because I weakened them. If it wasn't for me, we wouldn't have the materials for this boat in the first place!"

"What do you mean 'pointy hat'?" Kat asked. "Like a witch's pointy hat?! As in . . . you got this sword from a witch?!"

"She wasn't a witch—she just had a triangle-shaped growth on her head!" Tai said defensively.

Kat was stunned. Her hands slipped off the steering wheel . . .

BUMP!

The side of the boat collided with the swampy riverbank. It lurched, then came to a standstill.

Kat tripped and fell onto her side.

"Oof!" She winced, rubbing her elbow. She didn't see the starstone fall out of her pocket.

Alex clung to Amby for stability.

"Whoa!" Tai stumbled back and fell over the side of the boat. They managed to grasp the side with one hand, but the sword slipped from Tai's other hand and dropped into the river.

"NO!" cried Tai.

Their friends rushed to help pull them up onto the boat. But as soon as Tai was back on board, they tried to reach over the side to grab the sword.

"Just let the sword go!" shouted Alex.

"Kat, why didn't you steer the boat better?!" wailed Tai.

"Your arguing distracted me!" replied Kat, trying to pull Tai away from the water. "And now your foolishness is distracting me!"

A strange fizzing noise began to drown out the gang's shouting. When they looked over the side of the boat, they saw the sword was giving off sparks as it sank, and then . . .

It exploded in a strange purple light.

Suddenly, Witchat flew up into the air on her broom.

"Wh-what the?!" stuttered Kat in shock.

Witchat swooped down and picked up the gang's instrument from the deck. "Oh, CK is going to LOVE this!" she said with a sharp-toothed grin.

"Don't tell me this is who gave you the sword, Tai..." muttered Alex.

"Sure did!" Witchat said with a wink. "But you know what's even more dangerous than that sword? The awful music you were making!" she cackled.

"That sword was draining Tai's stamina, wasn't it?" asked Alex flatly.

Witchat nodded. "YEP! Also, the eye on it let me spy on you through my crystal yarn ball."

"Why are you spying on us?! What do you want?!" demanded Kat.

Witchat yawned and batted at her crystal yarn ball. "Calm down, kid," said Witchat. "I'm just doing

this for the paycheck. It's my BOSS who hates you, and I can see why. You've been gathering way too many resources, which is a no-no in his kingdom!"

"HIS kingdom?" said Kat, Alex, and Tai.

"Hold on." Witchat held her wand to her ear like a phone. "I think he wants to talk to you . . ."

Witchat shouted from her broom. "Bow down to the Craft King!"

CHAPTER 8

The Craft King's booming, maniacal laugh echoed around the boat.

"You really thought you could get away with it, didn't you?" said the Craft King.

"Uh . . . Get away with what exactly?" asked Tai.

"I WON'T FALL FOR YOUR FOOLISH TRICKERY!" the Craft King roared.

"Um, to be fair, sire," Witchat whispered to the king, "that one is more the type to fall for foolish trickery than create it. You should've seen them fall for that cursed sword—"

Tai's eyebrows furrowed.

"SILENCE!" the Craft King snarled. "The rules are

the rules!! These little troublemakers broke them, and now they must face the consequences!"

"Troublemakers?" Tai looked around in confusion.

"We have no idea what 'rules' you're even talking about!" protested Kat.

"What do you mean?! I put signs up everywhere! Or at least . . . I ordered them to be put up everywhere," the Craft King said, eyeing Witchat.

"B-but, sire, you hadn't approved the design yet!" stuttered Witchat.

"SHOW THEM THE SAMPLE!" yelled the Craft King.

Witchat nodded rapidly and waved her wand . . .

The gang stared at the sign in quiet disbelief.

"'I DO NOT SHARE'? Are you sure my two-year-old sister didn't write this?" asked Kat. "Actually, even she has better manners than this!"

Alex and Tai laughed.

The Craft King's eye twitched. But then a wide, toothy grin spread across his face. "Funny, is it?" he asked as he began to take giant, heavy steps toward the group.

Amby moved in front of Alex, Kat, and Tai protectively.

"When people don't share . . . when people hide things from one another . . . you think that's amusing, do you?" asked the king. He glanced at Witchat. "Why don't we show these three what their so-called friend has been hiding from them?"

"What?" Tai asked.

Alex was confused, too. "What is he talking about, Kat?"

Even Amby tilted her head in a question.

"I have no idea!" Kat said. But then she felt around in her pockets and realized . . .

"Oh no!" The starstone was lying on the deck where she'd dropped it.

"Oh yes," the Craft King said. His grin spread even wider. "Bring it to me."

Kat sprinted toward the gem, but before she could grab it, Witchat waved her wand and the stone flew from the deck into the Craft King's claws.

Tai's jaw dropped. "A starstone?! Where did it come from?"

"Why don't you explain, Kat?" said the Craft King with a smirk. "Oh, and while you're at it, you should tell them how long you've had it and why you waited so long to tell them!" His booming laughter echoed around the boat.

"He's lying, right?!" asked Alex.

Kat couldn't look her friends in the eyes. "I found it on the beach... I've had it the whole time."

"All right, I've had my fun," said the Craft King. "Witchat, bring everything to my castle: The starstone, the boat, and that unusual creature. Those horns will look pretty good up on my mantelpiece..."

"No!!" cried Alex, throwing his arms over Amby protectively. "You're not taking her!"

Alex heard a voice in his head. *Alex, I'll be okay...*

But as soon as Witchat waved her wand, the ornadeer disappeared in a puff of smoke.

Tai and Alex were speechless.

"Give her back!" Alex charged at Witchat.

With another wave of Witchat's wand, Alex, Kat, and Tai floated up into the air.

"What do you want to do with them?" asked Witchat. "I'll admit, they've got some pretty funny ideas—check this out!" She picked up their instrument and began to play it.

The Craft King winced, covering his large pointy ears. "Stop that AT ONCE!!"

Witchat stopped playing, her eyes wide with shock.

After taking a moment to recover, the Craft King cleared his throat. "Bring that thing back to the castle. It'll be perfect for making my enemies suffer. As for the brats..." The Craft King's evil grin was back. "Banish them to the meteor crater!"

Kat, Alex, and Tai could only watch helplessly as Witchat waved her wand once again, and...

Everything went dark.

CHAPTER 9

THUD!

Kat, Alex, and Tai fell to the hard, dirty ground.

"Ow!" Tai rubbed their elbow.

Alex sat up and looked around. Where was Amby?

The towering walls of the deep, dark crater surrounded them, but the ornadeer was nowhere to be seen.

Alex took out the shard of Amby's horn and stared down at it, his eyes welling with tears.

"She's . . . gone."

Tai rose to their feet with clenched fists. Then suddenly they sprinted toward the crater wall and desperately tried to climb it, but it was too steep and they slipped. Tai was so tired, but they kept trying to find a way out.

Kat hurried over to Tai. "Stop, you're going to hurt yourself—"

"Oh, NOW you care about helping?" Tai snapped.

"None of this would have happened if you'd been honest, Kat," said Alex, his voice strained.

Kat backed away, then sat on the ground. "I guess I thought if I told you guys about the starstone, you would've wanted to use it for yourselves," she said softly. "Tai, you would've wanted to make the best weapon ever. And Alex, you would've made it into food for some creature. You wouldn't have listened to any of my ideas!"

"That's really hypocritical," said Alex.

Tai nodded. "Yeah, that's hippo—" They paused. "Hippo what?"

"It means she did the thing she's accusing us of wanting to do," said Alex.

"I knew that," Tai responded.

"Kat, when you were making the boat, you didn't listen to any of my ideas at all," said Alex. "And neither of you believed me about Amby. She saved us back there! And we let her down."

"I didn't mean to," said Kat.

But Alex wasn't done. "I feel like you're lying about why you kept the starstone. Just like when you lied this morning."

Tai took a sharp breath. "This morning feels like forever ago. We don't even know how long we've been here."

"Do you think our families are looking for us?" asked Alex.

Thinking of her parents made Kat's heart sink

even lower. She hugged her knees. "We could be trapped in Otherworld forever..."

A long moment passed where no one said anything. Then Kat shook her head and rose to her feet. "Alex, you're right," she said. "I kept the starstone because I wanted to win the competition. I wanted to prove to myself that my hard work was worth it and my ideas were great... even if no one else agreed."

"Your ideas *are* great," said Alex. "But so are ours."

"They are," she said. "This adventure has shown me that there is no one right way to play. I should've been thinking about how to help all of us, and not just thinking of myself and what I wanted. I'm sorry."

"You're not the only one who should apologize," said Tai. They looked at the empty sheath where the cursed sword had been. "I can't believe I was so gullible. I trusted that witch and made that deal without asking you guys. I lost the starstone *and* Amby. I wanted to be the hero, but I should've been working with you guys, not some witch! I'm sorry, too."

Alex stared into the distance. "It felt like you didn't care about Amby at all. But I'm sorry I got so mad that I forgot to warn you guys about the sunken boat. That wasn't fair."

"You didn't do it on purpose," said Kat.

"No, but all I could think about was Amby," said Alex. "I know you like different parts of the game more, and that's okay. You're great with weapons, Tai. And Kat, your craft ideas are awesome!"

"It's so cool that you know so much about creatures," Kat replied. "That's what makes us a great team."

Tai nodded. "Amby is part of that team, too. She really kicked zombie butt back there!"

Alex smiled, then looked down at the horn

fragment in his hand. "So how are we gonna get her back? The walls of the crater are too slippery to climb."

Tai picked up a handful of dirt and sifted it through their fingers. "And there are no materials here either."

Alex held up Amby's horn fragment to the sky. It glinted in the moonlight and caught Kat's eye.

"That's it!" she said with a snap of her fingers. "Alex, can I please borrow that?"

"Sure!" he said, handing the shard to Kat. "But what for?"

Kat began to dig at the ground with the sharp piece of horn. "If this is a meteor crater, like the king said, then there's a chance we could find meteor rocks to craft with!"

Alex gasped. "You're right!"

Tai cheered and punched the air. "You really do have great ideas, Kat!"

She grinned and kept digging. When her arm got

tired, Alex offered to help. Kat gave him the shard and he dug for as long as he could. When Alex was exhausted, he handed it to Tai to take over. And when Tai ran out of energy, they passed the shard back to Kat.

They kept passing it between one another and digging until . . .

CLINK!

A brilliant light glowed at the bottom of the hole.

The three friends reached down together and pulled out . . . a starstone fragment!

"What?!" said Kat. "A starstone means this isn't a meteor crater at all." She looked around, taking in the five walls that surrounded them. "It's a falling star crater!"

"The Craft King should NOT have dropped us here," Alex laughed.

"WAHOO!" shouted Tai. "We should keep looking for more pieces, right?"

Alex and Kat nodded. So they continued to dig. But they couldn't find anything else.

"Too tired to keep going . . ." Alex slumped to the ground.

Kat brushed dirt off her knees. "That's okay. The single piece we already have will be enough to craft anything we can think of!"

"We just have to remember that whatever we make will run out after a while," Alex reminded them.

"Right!" said Kat. "Still, we could make a giant

Alex and Tai beamed at her.

"Something that we only can make together!" said Alex.

And so, they began to craft.

slingshot, or a massive trampoline, or a rocket..."
She paused and looked at her friends.

CHAPTER 10

It was a peaceful night in Otherworld. The crickets chirped and the wind whistled through the trees.

Then suddenly...

With a loud boom like a clap of thunder, a shooting star blasted across the sky over the mountain range. Then it shot down, heading straight toward the Craft King's castle.

With another **BOOM!** the star broke straight through the door.

The Craft King jumped up from his golden throne.

In a cage by his side, Amby scrambled to her feet.

Once the dust settled... the intruders were revealed.

"How dare you break down my gate!" bellowed the Craft King.

"Yo, it's us again! Surprised?" Tai waved from their seat of the team's epic invention: a huge robot with antlers and a giant sword.

The robot waved at the Craft King, too.

Amby brayed in delight.

The Craft King backed away. "Wh- . . . but . . . how?!"

Kat smirked. "You kindly dropped us in a shooting star crater, and we found a fragment. Thanks for that!"

"Meet MECHADEER!" declared Alex.

The Craft King's eye twitched as he stared at the robot. "This design is ridiculous! And a complete waste of materials! What am I even looking at?!"

"Our strengths combined!" shouted Kat, while Tai drove toward Amby's cage so Alex could pull open the bars with the power of robotic antlers and free her. Then Tai turned the mechadeer toward the Craft King. The robot towered over him.

The Craft King glared up at them. "You really think you can get away with stealing from me? You don't think I've spent every moment planning for this?"

"A giant robotic deer breaking into your house?" asked Tai with a raised eyebrow. "Yeah, I would be surprised if you had planned for that."

"GUESS AGAIN!" roared the Craft King. He grabbed the golden statues and gold-framed portraits of himself and tore them apart until he had a pile of gold blocks at his feet. He ripped his golden throne from the ground, and within moments, he had crafted . . .

THE GOLDEN ARMOR!!

The Craft King pointed one of his giant golden swords. "Try me, you overconfident little fools."

"Did the guy with the giant statues of himself just call *us* overconfident?" asked Kat.

"You're going down!" declared Tai. The mechadeer charged at the Craft King. "We won't give in until we win!"

But then the lights on the mechadeer's control panel turned off.

"Oh no!" said Alex. "The starstone fragment's lost power!"

As soon as the words were out of his mouth, the

mechadeer shattered into a thousand tiny stars that rained down through the air and disappeared.

Kat, Alex, and Tai were right behind them. But just before they hit the ground . . .

. . . Amby caught each of them on her back.

"THANK YOU, AMBY!" said Tai. They wrapped

their arms around Amby in a hug. "I'm so sorry I nearly traded you!"

Don't mention it, said a mysterious voice in Tai's mind.

Tai's eyes went wide. "W-who said that?!"

The Craft King laughed mockingly. "I have access to every material and monster in this land. How could you possibly expect to defeat *me*? If I wanted to, I could summon an army of zombies to finish you off right now..."

The kids glanced at one another nervously.

"But after all the trouble you've caused," the king continued, "I'd rather destroy you with my own hands." Faster than a shooting star, he crafted both his arms into two giant cannons that he pointed down at Kat, Alex, Tai, and Amby.

As the Craft King began to charge the power of his cannons, the kids heard a voice inside their heads.

The Monstrosity. You need to use the Monstrosity!

Alex gasped at Amby. "That was you, wasn't it, Amby?"

The ornadeer nodded and spoke again. *He would never think to take it because it's something only you three could create together!*

Kat gasped. "She's right! Remember earlier? He couldn't stand the sound!"

Tai pointed to the other side of the room, where the instrument lay on the ground. "It's over there!"

Alex nodded. "Let's go, Amby!"

Amby sprinted across the hall, the kids clutching her fur to stay aloft.

"There's no escape!" boomed the Craft King, his cannons close to fully charged.

Kat reached over and grabbed the Monstrosity. Just before the Craft King fired, she and her friends jumped off Amby's back and began to play their instrument as badly and as loudly as they could.

The Craft King's armor began to break apart, and

the starstone dropped from his pocket and fell to the ground. Amby dashed for it and brought it back to the trio as the castle walls began to rumble . . .

Kat stopped playing. "With the Craft King weakened, everything he's crafted is falling apart!"

"We've got to get out of here or we're going to be crushed!" cried Tai.

Everyone jumped onto Amby's back. Alex steered her around falling blocks and platforms.

Soon, they managed to escape. From the mountainside, they watched the castle collapse into rubble behind them.

"That was close!" Alex said.

"But there's the portal!" Kat pointed. It was closer than ever.

"How are we going to get all the way up there?" asked Tai, scratching their head.

"I think I have an idea," Kat said with a smile. She pulled the starstone from her pocket.

But it had shattered into pieces!

"Oh no!" cried Alex. "What are we going to do now?"

"It's okay," said Kat, handing both Alex and Tai a piece. "I'll use this fragment to make a bridge. But we'll have to hurry across it before it shatters. You guys can keep your pieces for the competition!"

"Are you sure, Kat?" asked Alex.

"Positive!" said Kat. She focused on her fragment and crafted a beautiful starry bridge that stretched all the way up to the sky.

"Wow, so cool!" said Tai.

Amby started up the bridge, with Alex, Kat, and Tai holding on tightly. But part of the way up, the ornadeer's ear twitched, and she spun around.

"What's wrong, Amby?" asked Alex. Then he gasped.

A hand burst out from the rubble of the castle. It was the Craft King. And his eyes were filled with fury.

When he was finally free, he raised his glowing palm.

Suddenly, an army of emberdead appeared... and began to run up the bridge!

CHAPTER 11

"Run, Amby, run!" cried Alex.

Amby scampered away from the emberdead as fast as she could.

Kat looked over her shoulder. The emberdead were scrambling up the bridge.

"You guys don't think they can cross through the portal with us . . . right?!" she asked nervously.

Tai took their starstone fragment out of their pocket. "Go ahead without me!" they declared, jumping off Amby's back.

The ornadeer slowed down and turned around.

"Tai?! What are you doing?!" shouted Alex.

Tai held their starstone piece up in the air. "Ever since this morning, I've been thinking about what weapon would work best against the emberdead. And now I can use that idea to make sure they don't follow us home!"

Tai transformed their starstone piece into a pale blue sword that glinted in the sun like an icicle, then rushed toward the fiery zombies.

"TAI!!" cried Alex and Kat in alarm.

With every slash of Tai's sword, the emberdead froze into blocks of ice. But there were dozens of them, and Tai could only focus on attacking a few at a time.

"We've got to help Tai!" cried Kat.

"Amby's got the best shot of defeating those zombies. And she listens to me," said Alex. "You should get to the bridge!"

"I won't leave you guys behind!" said Kat. "But my inventory is empty. What can I do?"

"I know! Catch!" said Alex. He tossed Kat the final star fragment. "Now is the time to use it!"

Kat shook her head. "But the points, the competition..."

She was too late. Alex and Amby had already charged into battle, knocking emberdead off the bridge with Amby's horns.

Kat looked down at the star piece.

"I need to help get these zombies out of here..." she said to herself. But how?

Kat looked down from the bridge for inspiration. Something caught her eye: the star crater they had been dropped into earlier. She remembered Witchat using her magical weapon to send them there.

"That's it!" Kat held up the star fragment and focused. It began to glow and transformed into a wand.

Kat was feeling proud of herself as an emberdead slipped by Amby and Alex.

"Watch out!" cried Alex.

Kat pointed the wand at the emberdead, used a spell to make it float into the air, and tossed it over the bridge.

"Woohoo!" cheered Kat. "This wand is amazing!"

She and her friends continued to fend off the emberdead mob until they'd defeated all of them.

"Take THAT!" cried Tai as they knocked the last frozen emberdead off the bridge. "We won!"

Kat was just about to start celebrating when she realized . . .

"The bridge! It's starting to fade!" she cried. The portal was shrinking, too. "We've got to leave. Now!"

Alex and Amby picked up Tai and Kat. Then Amby ran for the portal as fast as her legs would carry them.

Tai glanced over their shoulder and spotted the Craft King charging up the bridge on all fours. "Uh-oh. We've got another problem!"

"YOU WON'T GET AWAY!" roared the Craft King.

Amby reached the top of the bridge and spun around.

The Craft King lunged at them. But just as he was

about to grab them with his claws . . . Kat immobilized him with her wand, Tai slashed him frozen solid with their sword, and Alex had Amby ram the ice block with her antlers.

The frozen block that was the Craft King rocketed all the way back down the bridge, slid over the rubble of his castle, and fell down the mountainside into the sea below with a **SPLASH!**

"We did it!" Tai cheered as everyone climbed off Amby's back.

"No more star fragments. I guess none of us are winning that competition, huh?" Kat joked.

"I'm just glad we're all safe," said Alex. "But you were right, Kat. We do make a great team."

"Yeah, we do." Tai nodded.

"What do you say we go home now?" Kat asked.

"But what about Amby?" Alex rested his hand on the ornadeer's head. "Are you going to be . . ."

He trailed off as Amby began to glow. Giant wings sprouted from her back, her hooves grew talons, and her tail spread out like a dragon's.

"Whoa!! Did she evolve again? She looks so cool!!" exclaimed Tai.

I am indeed cool. Amby's voice echoed in their heads. *Don't worry about me. I'll be okay. When this bridge disappears, I'll fly to safety.*

"I'll miss you," Alex said, eyes tearing up. He gave Amby a hug. Soon Tai and Kat joined in.

Thank you all for saving me. Now it is time you save yourselves. Amby nudged them forward with her nose. *Go, before the portal closes!*

"Everybody ready?" Kat asked breathlessly, offering Tai and Alex her hands.

They both nodded and grabbed on tight.

The friends took one final look back at Otherworld, then stepped through the portal . . . together.

CHAPTER 12

"All right, all right, settle down, everyone," said Mr. Garcia from the stage of the auditorium.

It was a week later. A week of classes and homework and Otherworld practice—the virtual kind. Kat, Tai, and Alex had spent a lot of time in the computer lab after school. They still disagreed from time to time. But their teamwork had never been better. And it had all led up to this: the Game Quest tournament fundraiser.

"Thank you to all of you who entered," said Mr. Garcia. "We managed to raise over five thousand dollars!"

The audience cheered so loudly the echoes bounced around the room.

Mr. Garcia waved a hand to quiet everyone. "And now for the moment I'm sure you've all been waiting for: It's time to announce the winners of the tournament."

The audience buzzed with whispers and murmurs.

"In third place... Matt Johannson!"

Matt waved at the audience as he walked up the stage steps and took his place on the winners' podium. Mr. Garcia looped a medal over his head.

"In second place, with a bonus award for best teamwork... it's Kat Baptiste, Alex Ortega, and Tai Zhang!"

In the audience, Kat, Alex, and Tai grinned at one another before hurrying up to the stage. Tai tripped on the bottom step but flashed a peace sign to let everyone know they were okay. Kat and Alex laughed at their friend's energy and followed them onto the podium. Mr. Garcia looped medals over each of their heads. Claps and whistles rang out from the crowd.

"And in first place . . ." said Mr. Garcia, pausing for dramatic effect, "our winner is Lucy Jackson!"

A roar of applause filled the hall as Lucy headed up the stairs. She twirled her hair and stood next to Kat, Alex, and Tai on the winners' podium.

Mr. Garcia smiled and handed her the trophy. "Congratulations, Lucy! Let's hear it for her and all of our winners, and all of you who participated!"

The crowd gave them a standing ovation.

"And now, I'd like to invite my favorite three-piece band to perform a song they wrote to celebrate this incredible day," said Mr. Garcia. "Give a big round of applause for . . . the Monstrosities!"

"Here we go," said Alex, grinning at Kat and Tai.

As they readied their instruments, Lucy leaned over to whisper, "I'd love to check out your server sometime!"

"Me too!" said Matt.

"Sure thing!" said Kat. "You guys can come over to my house this weekend."

Then it was time to jam. The trio began to play, drowning out all conversation.

Everybody winced from the awful sound, except Mr. Garcia.

Tai shrugged. "I think our music is growing on everyone!"

After the awards ceremony, Kat, Alex, and Tai headed to the computer lab.

"Are you guys ready?" asked Alex, his voice a little shaky.

Kat put her hand on Alex's back. "I'm sure she's okay."

"Yeah," agreed Tai. "Otherworld might be a dangerous place, but she's the best fighter I've ever seen. Apart from me, of course..."

The group sat down at their computers and logged on. They watched in silence as the Otherworld home screen loaded, waiting... waiting... until—

They heard the flapping of wings and the sound of hooves.

Everyone's face lit up! It was time to head back into Otherworld, for their next quest...

DON'T MISS THE NEXT GAME QUEST ADVENTURE!

The blades of swords locked, sending sparks flying. Tai pushed back against Maxi, waiting for an opening. But Maxi wasn't letting his guard down—he blocked Tai's every attack.

"Spinning attack!" shouted Tai. They spun their frost sword around quickly like a tornado.

"Too slow!" said Maxi, dodging Tai's sword. He smirked as Tai spun past him and into some nearby bushes. Tai jumped back out, swaying with dizziness, but steadied themself and ran back toward Maxi.

To Tai, this battle felt like life or death . . . But this was Otherworld, Tai's favorite video game in the Game Quest universe. Tai's hit points dropped with every slash from Maxi.

"You can do it, Tai!" Kat cheered from the sidelines, where her avatar waved along with Alex's. But Kat's encouragement was drowned out by the cheering of Maxi's fans.

Maxi was using Otherworld's new streaming feature, and his chat window kept chiming with messages from his fans from across the world.

Maximus is gonna win!
Go, Maxi!

Each ping seemed louder than the last.

PING!

Tai's eyes darted across to the chat window. They spotted a comment that read: *This Tai kid's got no chance! They're not as good as Maxi!*

Tai felt their heart sink.

THWACK! With Tai distracted, Maxi lunged and went for the final blow. Tai's hit points reached zero. They staggered back and fell onto the ground. "Oof!" The giant GAME OVER text appeared on-screen.

When Tai respawned, Maxi stuck out his hand. "You remember the bet, right? I get that frost sword of yours."

Tai looked down at the sword. "R-right." Tai slowly handed over their beloved frost sword.

Maxi snatched the sword and held it above his head, its blade sparkling in the light. "Nice, I'll add this to my collection!"

Tai's eyebrows furrowed. Collection? This was

Tai's *only* sword. They had made it themself thanks to a starstone, the rarest item in the game. Tai had only agreed to hand it over because they were so sure they would win. But now Tai had no idea when they could ever get their hands on anything like it again.

Kat and Alex walked over. "Good job, both of you! Maxi, you were amazing!" said Kat.

"Yeah, I've never seen someone fight like that before. Your skill is on another level," Alex added.

"I always love to entertain my fans!" Maxi said, striking a pose. "Even if that means kicking a friend's butt in the process." He laughed.

Maxi's chat filled with laughing emojis.

Tai's face turned red. Maxi and his chat, which was basically the whole world, were laughing at them. Tai's dream of battling their idol had turned into a nightmare!

Back in the real world, Tai sat with their laptop on the table, staring at the screen in disbelief.